A Turkey Drive
and Other Tales

By BARBARA ANN PORTE

Pictures by YOSSI ABOLAFIA

Greenwillow Books, New York

Library of Congress Cataloging-in-Publication Data

Porte, Barbara Ann.
  A turkey drive and other tales / by Barbara Ann Porte;
pictures by Yossi Abolafia.
        p.   cm.
  Summary: A sister and brother who enjoy storytelling
like their father and art like their mother join in making
up stories about different pictures around their house.
  ISBN 0-688-11336-2
  [1. Storytelling—Fiction.   2. Family life—Fiction.]
I. Abolafia, Yossi, ill.
PZ7.P7995Tu   1993
[Fic]—dc20
91-48032   CIP   AC

FOR YOSSI,

WITH LOVE

I'm Abigail. My brother is Sam. We live with our mother and father and a small dog named Benton. Our mother is an artist. She draws and paints at home. Sam and I do, too.

Our father drives a taxicab. When he comes home from work, he often tells us stories. Sometimes his stories go with our pictures.

"It's called art appreciation," Daddy says.

"Really?" says Mom, listening. Sam and I listen, too. Even Benton pays attention. He also likes art.

A TURKEY DRIVE

One evening after dinner, Mom showed us her newest painting. It was a watercolor of two birds standing in a grassy field. There were trees in the background.

"I like your painting," said Daddy. "It reminds me of a turkey drive."

"A turkey drive?" said our mother. So did Sam and I. Even Benton looked interested.

"Right," said our father. "I haven't heard of

one in years. But when my father was Sam's age, turkey drives were a yearly event. Grandpa used to tell me about them."

"Your father drove turkeys when he was Sam's age?" Mom sounded surprised.

"Not *drove* them. Driving turkeys was a grown person's job. My father just watched," Daddy said.

"I see," said our mother. She began clearing the table.

Sam and I didn't see. Daddy was glad to explain.

"Sure," he said. "They drove turkeys to town the same way as cows. Almost the same. They were farmers who drove them, not cowboys. It was easy to tell by their hats. Also, no one rode horses. Everyone walked, including the turkeys.

A farmer or two would round up his own and all of the neighbors'. A couple of hundred turkeys made a pretty good drive. An early start was the main thing they needed."

"An early start?" Sam asked.

"Oh, yes," Daddy said. "A turkey is not like an owl. Turkeys do not care to be out after dark. When sundown comes, they pull off the road, find themselves trees, and roost for the night. A person can just hang up his hat then. There's nothing a driver can do to get them back on the road before morning. Some turkey drives took two or three days. That was some sight, believe me—high-stepping turkeys strutting along, not a care in the world except foxes." Daddy smiled, remembering.

"Foxes?" said Mom. She'd been busy scraping leftovers into Benton's bowl, but stopped to look up.

"Sure," Daddy said. "Foxes are the main
reason turkeys like roosting. Sitting still in a tree
in the dark makes it hard for foxes to find you,
even foxes with very good eyesight."

"Well, sure, eyesight," said Sam. "But aren't
turkeys birds? Why can't they just fly away from
a fox?" I'd been wondering the same thing
myself.

"Ah," said Daddy. "You're thinking of wild
turkeys. The ones on the drive were all tame.

Tame turkeys have their wing feathers clipped at the elbows to keep them at home. Also, they're usually too fat to fly far.''

''That's all very interesting, but I really don't see what it has to do with my picture,'' said Mom. She looked first at Daddy, then at her painting. ''My birds are pheasants, not turkeys. They're standing still in a field, not strutting. There isn't even a driver in view.''

Daddy peered again at Mom's painting. ''You

know, you could be right," he said. "Though it's hard to tell from this distance. A pheasant seen from afar can look like a turkey, or the other way around. I think the pair in your picture were probably at the tail end of the drive, lagged behind, and got lost. See how they're looking about trying to decide which way to go. It's a good thing there are so many trees. Now they can roost for the night. By the time the drivers get to town, count their turkeys, and find two are missing, it will be too late to go back."

"What will happen to Mom's turkeys then?" asked Sam.

"Don't worry, the weather is still warm. They'll be fine," Daddy told him. "By the time winter comes, they'll be thinner, with longer wing feathers. They'll find a flock of wild turkeys to join, and fly free. They'll be much better off that way, believe me."

"Really?" said our mother.

The next day, when Sam and I got home from school, Mom's painting was hanging, framed, in the foyer.

2

SAM'S ROOSTER

I don't know whether it was seeing Mom's pheasants hanging in the hallway, or just that Sam liked birds himself, but one day, not long after Mom had hung her painting, Sam came home from school carrying a picture of a rooster he had made in Art.

It was a tall rooster, with a red comb on its head and a fancy, feathery tail. It was standing on both feet, leaning forward on its toes, its

mouth wide open, crowing. You could tell that
rooster was proud of itself. Sam was proud of his
picture. "See, that's the sun coming up," he said,
pointing to a red crayon circle just behind the
rooster.

"Nice work, Sam," Mom told him. Sam was
pleased to hear it. After all, if anyone would
know, wouldn't it be our mom?

"It's a good job," Daddy said when he saw it.
Then he looked harder at the picture and cleared

his throat. "I wonder why your rooster isn't facing east, looking at the sun. Whenever mine crowed, that's what they did."

"I beg your pardon," said Mom. "Whenever your *what* crowed?"

"My roosters," said Daddy.

"I didn't know you ever had roosters," I said.

"Oh, sure, when I was your age I did," Daddy said. Then he explained: "I ordered them from a Sears, Roebuck catalog. A hundred baby chicks cost ten dollars. They came boxed in the mail. I

raised them in our living room until they were big enough to sell."

"Who did you sell them to?" Sam asked.

"Whoever wanted to buy them," Daddy answered. "Chickens make very good pets," he added in a while.

"Chickens? I thought you said roosters," I said.

"Right," Daddy said. "It's hard to tell when they're newborn. Out of every batch of chicks, about half will turn out hens, the other half roosters. You don't know which are which until their combs start growing in. 'Ah, rooster,' you say then. Pretty soon after, mine would begin running out of doors every morning, flapping their wings, squinting at the sun, and crowing in chorus. I knew then it was time to sell them. 'So much noise,' the neighbors would say, coming by in the evening, complaining."

Before Sam went to sleep that night, he taped his picture onto the refrigerator door. He'd added a title, carefully printed at the bottom: CROWING ROOSTER FACING WEST. "See, this way it doesn't have to squint," he told us.

The next morning when I came into the kitchen, Benton was sitting in front of the refrigerator, squinting up at the picture. I think he'd never seen a rooster before.

The following weekend we visited Grandpa. Sam checked on Daddy's story. "So far as I know, whichever way a rooster happens to be facing, that's the way it crows," Grandpa told us. "Including your father's." Sam was glad to hear it.

3

RELEASING PIGEONS

"Speaking of birds," Daddy said one morning at breakfast, though nobody had been, "I know a Chinese story about pigeons."

Mom sighed. "Really?" she said.

"It's a very short story," Daddy told her.

"I didn't know they had pigeons in China," said Sam.

"Sure they have them, only they're called turtledoves," explained Daddy. Then he told us this story.

"Once upon a time, in a certain province in China, every year just before the New Year, the king offered a reward to whoever caught and brought him pigeons. The king wanted the pigeons so that he could release them in a special New Year ceremony. As you can imagine, the people spent quite a bit of time at the end of every year capturing as many pigeons as they could to carry to the king. Unfortunately, every year, as careful as the people were, some of the pigeons got hurt in the process."

"Why did the king want to release so many pigeons in the first place?" Sam asked.

"Ah," said Daddy. "That's exactly what the

boy in the story asked his father. His father was very busy at the time trying to catch pigeons, but even so, he stopped to explain. 'The reason the king releases pigeons every New Year is to show the people what a kind and gentle ruler he is,' the father in the story explained to his son."

"That sounds pretty stupid to me," I said. "If the king didn't give rewards for pigeons to begin with, the people wouldn't catch them, and the birds would be free all along."

"That's exactly what the girl in the story said," Daddy replied. "'If the king really wanted the pigeons to be free, he'd make it be against the law for anyone to ever catch one,' she told her father. Her father agreed. 'But, see, the king has never thought of it that way. Which goes to show that even a king can't think of everything,' the father in the story told his daughter."

"I thought you said it was a boy in the story talking to *his* father," Sam said.

Daddy looked puzzled. Then he understood what Sam meant. "Right. It was a boy in the story who asked, 'Why?'—but it was his sister who pointed out what was wrong with the answer. Which goes to show two heads can be better than one," Daddy said. Then he stood, reached for his cap, and kissed Mom, Sam, and me good-bye. "Time to go to work," he said.

"Time to go to school," we said.

Mom stayed home to paint, as usual. Benton stayed with her.

4

A VERY FORGETFUL PERSON

When Sam and I got home from school, Mom had just finished working. She showed us her picture. It was of a man lying in a hospital bed, wrapped in white bandages. A rope attached to a pulley was holding up one of his legs.

"It's in traction. He broke it," Mom said. She was getting ready to go out. "I have to run to the store for some paintbrushes. I'll take Benton along. He can use the exercise." Benton looked surprised to hear it, but ran to get his leash. "I'll be back soon. Be good, fix yourselves snacks, lock the door behind me, and don't let anybody in. If Daddy gets home before I do, he has a key," Mom said. Then she kissed us good-bye and left with Benton. I locked the door behind them.

"Do you want to know how Mom's man broke his leg and ended up in the hospital?" I asked Sam as we were having milk and cookies in the kitchen. Sam did, so I told him.

"He was a very forgetful man. Every morning as he was getting ready to go to work, his wife asked him, 'Do you need your hat? Do you have your lunch? Did you take your key so you can get into the house if I'm not here when you get back?' She usually was, since she was a potter and worked at home.

"'Yes, yes, yes,' the man answered every day. 'But I wish you wouldn't ask me so many

questions all the time. It makes me nervous.'

"'Yes, dear,' the man's wife answered every morning. Then they always kissed each other good-bye, the man petted the dog, and he went out the door, whistling.

"One morning, however, the man's wife had a very busy day ahead of her and forgot to ask her husband anything. Instead, she only said, 'Good-bye, dear, have a nice day.' They kissed, the man petted the dog, and he left.

"As soon as he was outside, however, he

noticed it was very breezy. He put his hand to his head. Ah, he'd forgotten his hat. Well, that's just one thing less to have to remember coming home, he told himself, and he walked along, whistling, until he reached his office.

"The man worked very hard in his office all morning. When it was time for lunch, he was very hungry. Unfortunately, when he opened his desk drawer to take out his lunch bag, he discovered he'd left it at home. There's nothing like a good walk to work up an appetite, the man told himself as he left his office and began walking home. The man liked to walk. Even so, he thought what a good thing it was he lived so near to where he worked. When he arrived home, he felt famished.

"Unfortunately, when the man put his hand into his pocket to take out his key, he discovered he'd left it inside the house that morning. He rang the doorbell. Nobody answered. No one was home. His wife had run out of clay and gone to the store to buy more. She'd taken the dog along for exercise.

"The man didn't know what to do. Both the front and the side doors were locked, and so were the windows. The man looked up and scratched his head, thinking hard. That's when he noticed that high on the second floor, above the porch, one bathroom window was a teensy bit open. It was a very narrow window, but even so, the man thought there'd be just enough room to squeeze through. It's a good thing I'm not fat, he told himself. Then he told himself that all he'd have to do was shinny up the porch pole, climb onto the porch roof, grab onto the windowsill, and pull himself through the opening. It's a good thing I was such a good pole climber in high school, thought the man.

"He wrapped both his hands tightly around the pole and did the same with his ankles. Slowly, slowly, he began inching up. He was almost at the top. Then, just as he was reaching out one hand to grab onto the roof railing, his other hand,

and both ankles, slipped, and he began sliding, faster and faster, back down the pole. By the time he landed on the ground, his arms and legs were all tangled and going in different directions. The man knew for sure he'd broken more than one bone in his body.

"Fortunately, just at that moment, the man's next-door neighbor came out of her house and saw what had happened. She ran back inside and dialed 911 for emergency. By the time the ambulance arrived, the man's wife had returned with the clay and also the dog. Dogs are not

allowed in ambulances, so the woman left the dog with the neighbor, climbed into the ambulance herself, and rode in the back with her husband. 'You should have called a locksmith,' she told him all the way to the hospital."

"That's what I would have done," said Sam.

"Yes, but see, the moral of the story is that man didn't have to. He could have gotten into his house with no trouble. The neighbor had a spare key. The man's wife always left it whenever she had to go out. 'My husband's so forgetful. He'd forget his head if it weren't screwed on,' she said every time she did."

"So why didn't the man just ask the neighbor for the key?" Sam asked.

"That's a good question. See, the man's wife had forgotten to tell her husband about the arrangement," I told Sam. Just at that minute, Mom got back with Benton. He was carrying her package in his mouth. "We were just discussing your picture," I said.

"Oh?" said Mom. "It's for an insurance magazine. Its caption is going to be 'Most accidents happen at home.'"

"That's just what I was telling Sam," I said.

"Really?" said Mom. Just then there was a loud knocking at the door. Benton dropped Mom's paintbrushes on the floor, began barking, and ran to look. Sam ran right behind him.

"It's Daddy!" Sam yelled. Mom went to the door and let Daddy in. He looked a bit tired.

"I'm glad you're home. I just locked all my keys in the cab. It's a good thing I keep spares in my dresser," he said. He kissed us all hello, then headed for the bedroom. "I think I'll take a nap before dinner," he told us.

5

SAM'S STORY

The day Sam stayed home from school with a cold, he finger painted. He showed me his picture. All of it was red. The paper was red, the table was red, the chairs all were red, and so were the lamp, the bowl on the table, and all the place settings. A bright red frog was perched on the arm of one chair.

"Why is everything red?" I asked. Sam was glad to explain.

"It's red *now*, but it didn't used to be. It used to be tan," he told me. "And I don't mean just this one room only. I mean the whole house and everything in it was tan. The walls were tan, the ceilings were tan, the floors were tan, the curtains were tan, and so was all of the furniture. Even the outside of the house was painted tan. The woman whose house it was liked tan. Well, she used to like tan. Even she was starting to get tired of it.

"One day the woman was on her way home from shopping. She had on her tan coat and tan hat. She was carrying a tan paper bag with groceries in it. Another woman was walking along, almost beside her. She was dressed all in red and was carrying a very large, red wicker basket.

"'What a pretty color that is,' the woman in tan said as the woman in red began to pass her.

"'Thank you,' said the woman holding the basket. 'I just bought it. It was too large to wrap, but I don't mind carrying it home this way. Just looking at it makes me feel cheerful.'

"Well, just looking at it made the woman in tan feel cheerful, too. I wouldn't mind carrying it, either, if it were mine, she said to herself as she reached her front door. She went inside and looked all around. 'Tan, tan, tan! It's enough already,' she told herself out loud.

"Very early the next morning, she got up, got dressed, ate breakfast, and went outside. She took the first bus going downtown." Sam stopped talking to catch his breath.

"I know what she did next," I said. "She went shopping and bought everything new in red. 'Please send it,' she told the salesperson. 'There's too much to carry.'"

"Oh, no, she didn't," said Sam. I could tell by his tone he didn't like my ending. "All that woman bought downtown was paint. Red paint. Then she took the bus home, changed her clothes, and went to work. She painted everything, inside and out. She painted her roof and her walls, her curtains and her floors, her table and chairs, her dishes and bowl, and even her silverware."

"You left out the frog. Did she paint the frog red, too?" I asked.

"Don't be silly, Abigail. You can't paint a frog. A frog is a living thing," Sam told me. "Besides, she didn't have to. It was a rare tomato frog from Madagascar, the same as at the zoo. It was red to start with, and anyway, it didn't move in until *after* the woman painted." Sam sneezed. Then he sneezed again.

"How's your cold?" Mom asked, sticking her head into the room just then.

"Fine. I feel much better," Sam said. He sneezed some more. Mom came closer and noticed his painting.

"Nice. It reminds me, though—I'm out of red. I meant to pick up some the other day at the store," she said.

"Maybe you can borrow some of Sam's," I said. Sam shook his head.

"I used up all of mine on this painting," he told us. Mom laughed.

"I'm not surprised. Next time I'm out, I'll pick up some for both of us," she told him.

"I'm out of red, too," I said.

"I'll buy enough for everyone. 'Red, red, red, nothing but red,' I'll tell the salesperson. 'You

can never have too much of such a happy color.'"
Then Mom touched Sam on his forehead. "You
feel fine to me. I think you can go to school
tomorrow," she said, and left the room,
humming.

THE FASTEST HORSE
IN THE WORLD

Sunday I drew a picture of a horse and taped it next to my bed. I said, "It probably isn't very good. It's supposed to be a horse."

"We can all see that," said Daddy.

"You can?" I said.

"Of course. I can even tell, from the way its

tail streams out behind it, that it's a very fast horse. It's probably Mongolian."

"Mongolian?" said Sam.

"Right," said Daddy. "Mongolian horses are possibly the fastest in the world. In fact, there was once a Mongolian horse so fast it got stolen."

"Really?" said Mom.

"Oh, yes," Daddy said. "That horse was so fast, no one who rode it could ever be caught. It belonged to a farmer. The farmer loved that horse, and the horse loved that farmer. Word of the horse's speed spread far and wide until even the Russian czar heard of it. He wanted that horse. 'I *need* that horse,' the czar told his soldiers. They took it for an order. One soldier even crossed the border, stole that horse, and gave it to the czar. The czar rewarded him. He gave that soldier the horse's weight in gold.

"Not long after, the czar, who already owned a lot of horses—some of them quite fast themselves—traded the Mongolian horse to the King of Persia in exchange for his youngest daughter. Marrying the princess had been the czar's plan all along. It was the reason he'd wanted the horse in the first place. He knew how much the King of Persia liked fast horses. Now everyone was happy. The soldier had his gold; the czar had his queen, and eventually some nice children as well; and the King of Persia owned the fastest horse in the world. They could all live happily ever after.''

''Wait a minute,'' said Mom. ''What about the farmer?''

''Ah, yes,'' said Daddy. ''The story doesn't tell that. It also doesn't mention how the horse felt. But if you ask me, I think this is what happened: The horse was not happy in Persia. It never forgot the farmer who'd raised it. It always longed to be back. One day it escaped. It was a

long, hard trip across mountains and steppes. The weather was unpredictable. Finally, though, the horse arrived home. How happy the farmer was to see it! Now they could live happily ever after, and they did."

"Yes," said Mom, "but what about the czar? Did he have to give his queen back to the King of Persia? And, if so, who kept the children? And whatever happened to the gold?"

"That's what we'd all like to know," said Daddy.

7

A FAMOUS PAINTING

There is a large painting of a boy holding a dog that hangs on the wall above our sofa in the living room. The boy is standing in a field. This is how he looks: He has blond curly hair, rosy cheeks, and blue eyes. He is wearing a red jacket with a white lace collar and brown trousers that are baggy. He also has on white socks and brown lace-up shoes. A black top hat is lying on the ground beside him. This is how the dog looks: It is all white, with floppy ears, a round brown nose, and round brown eyes. Its hair is very wiry. It is probably some kind of terrier. The picture looks very old fashioned.

It was a present from Grandpa. He gave it to us when he moved from his old house into a new, much smaller apartment.

"I don't have room anymore for such a large painting. I thought you might like having it," he told Mom the day he drove here with it in his car.

"Oh, yes, thank you. I certainly would," she told him.

"That's me when I was Sam's age," Grandpa has told us many times since.

"Really?" Sam asked the first time.

"Sure. I'm almost bald now, but see, I had curly hair then, and so did my dog Whitey." Grandpa pointed toward the dog in the painting.

"I didn't know you had a dog," I said.

"You didn't?" Grandpa sounded surprised. "That was some dog, believe me. One time he saved my sister Eulalia from almost drowning. She was just a toddler then. I wasn't much older. We were both too young at the time to remember, but our father told us what happened. He'd heard all about it from our mother, your great-grandma.

"There was a terrible storm. Water came down in buckets, he told us. It made a large puddle in front of the house. After the rain had stopped, Eulalia and I went outside. Eulalia's boots were too big. She tripped and fell into that puddle, facedown. She was too surprised to get up or even

turn over. I was too surprised to help. Whitey,
who was just a puppy himself at the time, saw
what had happened. He started to bark. He
barked and barked until our mother came
running. She picked up Eulalia, held her upside
down, and hit her on her back until all the water

came out. Then she wiped Eulalia off and put her in dry clothing. 'What a good dog you are,' our mother told Whitey, over and over again, and she gave him a bone with the meat still on it for dinner.''

"Did that really happen?'' I asked.

"That's what your great-grandfather said. 'You can't be too careful in a downpour,' he always warned us. Why would he make up such a story?'' Grandpa asked.

A few weeks ago, a repairman came to our house to fix our television set. When he saw the painting in our living room, he stopped and stared. Then he shook his head and went to work on the television. Even as he worked, he glanced now and then at the painting. Just before he left, he said, "When I was growing up, we had that

same picture in our house. My parents still have
it. They live in the Philippines."

"Really?" said our mother. She sounded only
a little surprised.

"The television repairman's parents have a
picture of Grandpa in their house in the
Philippines?" Sam said as soon as the man was
gone. Sam sounded astonished. Mom smiled at
him.

"It isn't *really* a picture of Grandpa," she told
him. "It's really a reproduction of a famous

painting from a private collection. I'm sure a lot of copies have been made and sold to people all over the world."

"I didn't think that picture was really of you," Sam told Grandpa the next time he visited. I explained about the television repairman and what Mom had told us.

"Ah," Grandpa said. "I see what the problem is. You thought I meant I posed for that picture. Did I ever say that? Of course I didn't. That picture was painted a long time ago. I'm not that old. What I meant was, that's exactly how I looked when I was Sam's age, and so did my dog Whitey."

Daddy laughed when Sam told him. "Do you think Grandpa really looked like that?" I asked. We three and Benton were standing in front of the painting.

"Who knows? It's what he always told me. There are no photographs of him as a child." Daddy stared awhile at the picture. "Anyway, it's certainly a cute little boy, and the dog reminds me of Benton."

"Benton? Benton is black," I said.

"Right, that's what I meant. Except for its color, that dog looks exactly like Benton." Benton

put his head to one side, as though trying to see better. He barked a few times and jumped up on Daddy.

8

A HOSPITAL VISIT

Yesterday when I was looking for something to read, I found a drawing stuck in the back of one of Mom's books. It was a pencil sketch of a small, pitiful-looking child lying in an enormous bed, his head propped on pillows. A thermometer was sticking out of his mouth. A water pitcher was on the table beside him, and there was a crank at the foot end of the bed. A second child, and a small dog, were standing next to the bed. They looked very healthy. They also looked worried.

"Sam, come here!" I called. "Look what I found." Sam came running, and so did Benton. I showed Sam the picture. "Look, that's you, and that's me and Benton visiting," I said. "Mom must have drawn this last year when you were in the hospital." Sam stared at the picture.

"I don't think so, Abigail," he said in a while. "Dogs are not allowed in hospitals."

"Of course they're not," I said. "That's why I had to smuggle Benton in, inside my book bag. We almost got caught when he barked on the elevator. 'Sssh! Please be quiet, please,' I told him. 'Barking's not allowed in a hospital.' Don't you remember how we used to take him everywhere when we first got him, even to the movies one time in my pocket?"

"I remember," said Sam. "We were always being told to leave. We got put out of almost every place we went, *except* for the hospital. Benton never visited me there, and neither did you. You were too young. You had to be older to visit. They always made you wait in the lobby. You hated waiting there."

"Right," I said. "But that was last year. See, it's later in this picture. I'm older now. I'd be allowed up."

Just then our mother passed by and looked over our shoulders. "Well, what do you know!" she said. "I wondered what had happened to that picture. I drew it last year when Sam was in the hospital. Abigail always looked so pitiful waiting in the lobby. Putting her in my picture made me feel better. Of course I put Benton in, too."

"Really?" I said. It made *me* feel better just hearing about it.

9

MOM'S DANCING SHOES

"Come here, look at this!" Mom called to
anyone this morning. She'd been cleaning out
closets, going through boxes. Daddy, Sam, and I
came upstairs. Benton came with us. Mom
showed us a picture. It was a small pencil
drawing, gone over in pink, of a pair of toe shoes.

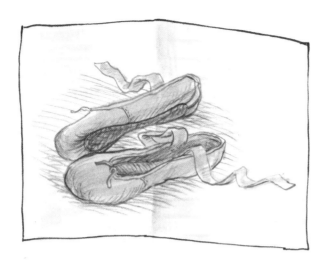

"I drew this when I was Abigail's age," she told us.

"It's very good," I said.

"I like it," said Sam.

Daddy stared at it a few minutes. Then he said, "Isn't that amazing?" He turned toward Sam and me. "See, it goes to show you can never start too early to plan for your future. Even way back then, Mom was already practicing to be an artist." Mom looked surprised to hear it.

"I was not," she said. "I'd been to see a ballet that day, *Swan Lake*. When I got home all I could think of was being a dancer. *That's* why I drew toe shoes. I wanted a pair, but my mother said no. 'Toe shoes damage your feet,' she told me. I didn't care. I begged and begged to take lessons. 'Absolutely not,' your grandmother said. Then she added, 'But you know, that's a very nice picture of dance shoes you've drawn. Perhaps you'd like to try art school.'

"'Absolutely not,' I told her. But later that year, my best friend Shirley moved away, and life was very boring. I started art class. After some time passed, I found that I liked it. That's when I began to think about being an artist."

That night, when Sam and I were already in our beds, I thought I heard music. I got up to look. I tiptoed over to the stairway and peered down through the railings. I saw Mom and Dad in the living room. The record player was on,

Mom was on her toes, and they were dancing. I woke Sam. He came with me to watch. Benton came, too. Daddy looked up and saw us.

"It's a waltz," he said. "Come on down." So we did. I danced with Sam. Then Mom and Dad took our hands and we all waltzed together. Benton got up on his hind legs, and tried waltzing, too.